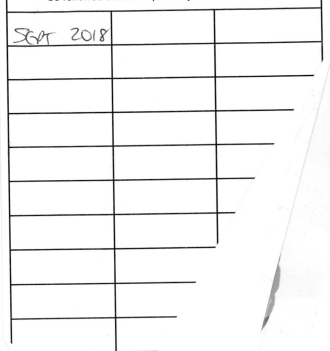

angry cookie

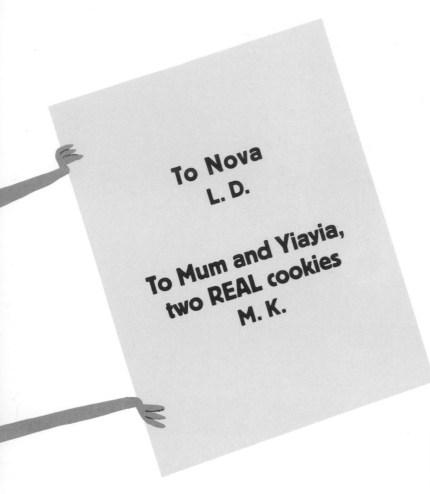

To Nova
L. D.

To Mum and Yiayia,
two REAL cookies
M. K.

First published 2018 by Walker Books Ltd
87 Vauxhall Walk, London SE11 5HJ

10 9 8 7 6 5 4 3 2 1

Text © 2018 Laura Dockrill · Illustrations © 2018 Maria Karipidou

The right of Laura Dockrill and Maria Karipidou to be identified as
author and illustrator respectively of this work has been asserted by them
in accordance with the Copyright, Designs and Patents Act 1988

This book has been typeset in Block T

Printed in China

British Library Cataloguing in Publication Data:
a catalogue record for this book is available from the British Library

ISBN 978-1-4063-6910-6

www.walker.co.uk

angry cookie

WALKER BOOKS
AND SUBSIDIARIES
LONDON · BOSTON · SYDNEY · AUCKLAND

LAURA DOCKRILL

MARIA KARIPIDOU

AGGGHH
It's so bright!
My eyes!
BALL
Close this book this very second, you nosy noodle!

And there is *nothing* you can do about it.

The end.

Errr ... Helllllloooo?

It all started yesterday
when my flatmate Barbra
(who is my cactus)
got out her new recorder.
She only knows this one terrible song and
keeps playing it over and over again.

I hate the recorder!

And you're not even allowed to
use the word hate.

But I just did...
So there.

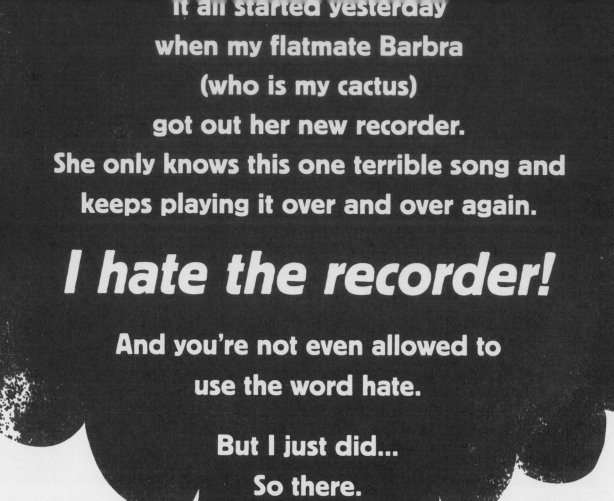

But they had run out of the
best, most wonderful
vanilla sundae
with hot caramel sauce
with whipped cream
and marshmallows
and a flake
with hundreds-and-thousands
and chocolate sprinkles
and *even* the red *cherry*...
They did have the tall glass.

On the way home a bird tried to *snack* on me. *"Get off! SHOO!"* I shouted.

But I don't think cookies often get heard.

Maybe *that's* why I'm so angry at the whole world?

Because *nobody* listens to me, nobody sticks around.

You keep coming back.